Seaside Mystery

To Ambrose, teddy-faced ginger tom.

GROSSET & DUNLAP
Published by the Penguin Group
Penguin Group (USA) Inc., 375 Hudson Street, New York, New York 10014, USA

USA | Canada | UK | Ireland | Australia | New Zealand | India | South Africa | China
Penguin Books Ltd, Registered Offices: 80 Strand, London WC2R 0RL, England

For more information about the Penguin Group visit penguin.com

Text copyright © 2007 by Sue Bentley. Illustrations copyright © 2007 by Angela Swan. Cover illustration copyright © 2007 by Andrew Farley. First printed in Great Britain in 2007 by Penguin Books Ltd. First published in the United States in 2013 by Grosset & Dunlap, a division of Penguin Young Readers Group, 345 Hudson Street, New York, New York 10014. GROSSET & DUNLAP is a trademark of Penguin Group (USA) Inc. Printed in the U.S.A.

Library of Congress Cataloging-in-Publication Data is available.

ISBN 978-0-448-46731-3   10 9 8 7 6 5 4 3 2 1

Magic Kitten

Seaside Mystery

SUE BENTLEY

Illustrated by Angela Swan

Grosset & Dunlap
An Imprint of Penguin Group (USA) Inc.

★ P r o l o g u e ★

The young white lion sped across the dusty plain. Flame knew that he must find some cover. It was too dangerous to be out in the open.

Suddenly a terrifying roar rang out, and an enormous black adult lion rose from a clump of tall grass and bounded toward him.

"Ebony!"

Flame leaped behind a huge rock. There was a dazzling white flash and where he once had stood now crouched a tiny, long-haired, brown tabby kitten with a bushy tail.

Flame's heart beat fast in his tiny chest as he backed slowly into a wide crack in the rock. His uncle Ebony was very close. He hoped this disguise would protect him.

The shadow of an enormous paw appeared, just inches away from the trembling kitten's little brown nose. Flame's emerald eyes sparked with fear and anger as he tensed his muscles, ready to fight.

"Stay where you are, Prince Flame. I will protect you," growled a deep but gentle voice.

Flame sank back in relief as an old gray lion peered in at him. "I am glad to see you again, Cirrus," Flame mewed. "But I do not think even you can protect me from my uncle. He is determined to keep the throne he stole from me, so he can rule in my place!"

Cirrus nodded gravely. "That is true. It is not safe yet for you to stay here. Use this disguise and go back again to the other world. Hide there until you grow strong and wise and then return to save our land from this evil."

The tiny kitten looked up into Cirrus's tired old face. "I will do as you say, old friend. Ebony will not rule forever!"

Cirrus's eyes flickered with affection. He reached a huge paw inside the crack in the rock and gently patted the tiny kitten's head. "And I cannot wait for that day. Go now, my prince," he growled softly.

Suddenly another mighty roar rang out. The ground shook as Ebony leaped onto the rock where Flame was hiding.

"Save yourself, Flame! Go quickly!" Cirrus urged.

Sparks glowed in the tiny kitten's long brown tabby fur. Flame mewed softly as he felt the power building inside him. He felt himself falling. Falling . . .

Chapter
ONE

"What an amazing view!" Maisie Simpson said excitedly. She leaned on her bedroom windowsill and peered out of the window.

Sunshine sparkled on the sea, and creamy waves washed onto the nearby sandy beach. Seagulls wheeled above the cliffs, soaring overhead in the clear blue sky.

Maisie and her parents had only just moved to the house in Bridhampton-on-Sea. She was dying to tell her two oldest friends, Jane and Nina, all about it. They had promised to keep in touch, even though Maisie would be living so far away. Maisie had hoped they would call her the night before, but neither of them had.

On impulse, she ran downstairs and called each of them in turn. There was no answer from Jane's home phone. Nina was out, too. Maisie left her a message on her answering machine.

They probably went swimming or are playing tennis, she told herself, trying not to care that they were having fun without her. It was school vacation, after all.

Maisie sighed. She squeezed past the boxes of books and china stacked in the hall and opened the door that led into the old candy store on the side of their house.

A loud banging sound met her ears as she went inside. Her dad was painting the walls and her mom was up on a ladder, putting up shelves. They were both artists and were busy turning the old store into a combined studio and gallery.

Karen Simpson stopped hammering
and looked down at her daughter.
"Hi, honey. You look sad. Is something
wrong?" she asked.

Maisie told her about calling Jane
and Nina. "They weren't around. And
they didn't call last night. Maybe they've
already forgotten all about me."

"What—in a couple of days? I don't
think so," her mom reasoned. "I bet
they're letting you settle in before they
call to check in. Why don't you try them
again later?"

Maisie nodded. "I will. It's just
that . . . I wanted to talk to them now."

Her mom came down the ladder.
"You're really missing your old friends,
aren't you?" she said, giving Maisie a
hug.

Maisie nodded, feeling a lump rise in her throat.

"It won't be long before school starts again, you know. And then you'll make lots of new friends. Am I right or am I right?"

Maisie managed a smile in response. But school didn't start for another two weeks. Right now, it felt more like two years.

James Simpson dropped his wet paintbrush into the open paint can. He winked at his daughter. "I've got a guy coming to set up the computer today. You'll be able to e-mail Jane and Nina to your heart's content tonight."

"Oh, that's great, Dad!" Maisie felt herself cheering up. She knew that her friends went online for a while most evenings. She would tell them all about her cool new house that had an old candy store attached to it!

"In the meantime, if you're bored, you could give me a hand with this painting," her dad suggested.

Maisie wrinkled her nose. Decorating was definitely not on her list of fun things to do!

"It's a lovely day and the beach looks

like it's calling your name," her mom said.

"Or you could—" her dad began.

"I think I will go exploring," Maisie decided quickly, before he thought of another job for her to do.

Mrs. Simpson chuckled. "Have a good time and don't go too far. Lunch will be ready in an hour or so."

"Okay, I'll be back by then," Maisie answered, heading for the door.

She went back through the house and out the back door. The small back garden was narrow and mostly paved, with plants in big decorative pots. Beyond the garden fence, the ground fell away steeply to the beach below.

Maisie opened the gate in the fence and went down the steep flight of stone steps. A warm breeze, smelling of salt,

ruffled her shoulder-length brown hair.
Once on the beach, she took off her shoes,
knotted the laces, and hung them around
her neck.

As she padded along, her toes sank
into the warm sand. She passed a family
with two small children flying a kite. At
the edge of the shore, where the waves
crashed onto the sand, three girls were
splashing around and laughing.

Maisie felt a flicker of loneliness. She
sighed as she wandered along the beach,
stopping now and then to pick up unusual
shells. After a few minutes, she reached the
rocks at the foot of the cliffs.

Shallow pools of water, left behind
by the outgoing tide, gleamed in the sun.
It was peaceful here with just the sound
of the waves and seabirds. The people on

the beach were only small specks in the
distance.

Maisie found a flat rock. She sat
down to dangle her bare feet in the cool
water below it as she thought about
how much fun Jane and Nina would be
having back home without her. Fronds
of delicate seaweed tickled her toes, and a

prawn scurried across the sandy bottom. Maisie was leaning forward to look at it when, in the reflection of the water, she suddenly saw a bright silver flash.

"Oh!" She twisted around in surprise. There, standing on a nearby rock, Maisie saw a tiny kitten. It had long brown tabby fur, a bushy tail, and the brightest emerald eyes she had ever seen. Its fur and whiskers seemed to be glowing with a thousand tiny sparkles of light.

Maisie frowned. Perhaps the kitten was wet for its fur to sparkle like that. The poor little thing did seem to be trembling as if it was cold.

"Hello," she crooned. "Where did you come from? What are you doing out here on the rocks, all by yourself?"

The kitten looked up at Maisie with wide, scared green eyes. "I come from far away. Can you help me, please?" it mewed.

Chapter
TWO

Maisie stared at the kitten in amazement. She must be even lonelier than she thought. She'd just imagined that the kitten had spoken to her!

Just then a seagull swooped down as if deciding whether the tiny tabby kitten would make a meal. The kitten cringed and yowled with fear.

Maisie jumped up and waved her

arms at the gull to scare it away. "Leave him alone!" she cried.

She went toward the kitten and bent down, so that it wouldn't get scared away.

"I wonder what your name is," she murmured, reaching out to stroke its trembling little body.

The kitten blinked up at her slowly,

and some of the fear seemed to fade from its eyes. Despite its tiny size, it didn't seem to be afraid of her.

"I am Prince Flame. What is your name?" it purred.

Maisie jerked her hand back. "Oh! You really *can* speak!" she gasped. "I'm . . . I'm Maisie Simpson. I just moved into a house near the beach with my parents." Her curiosity began to overcome her shock. "Did you say *Prince* Flame?"

Flame nodded and lifted his tiny head proudly. "I am heir to the Lion Throne. My uncle Ebony has stolen it and rules in my place. He is fierce and cruel and sends his spies to find me and kill me."

Maisie shook her head, trying to take it all in. Could everything this tiny cute kitten said be true?

Flame seemed to know what she was thinking. He moved sideways across the rocks away from her.

"Stay back," he ordered.

There was a blinding silver flash and for a moment Maisie couldn't see anything. But when her sight had cleared, the kitten had disappeared and in its place a majestic, young white lion stood proudly on the rocks.

Maisie gasped, scrambling backward on her hands and knees. "Flame?"

"Yes. It is me, Maisie. Do not be afraid," Flame said in a deep velvety roar.

Before she could say anything, there was another bright flash and instantly Flame was a fluffy, long-haired kitten once more.

"I guess it's all true," Maisie murmured.

"I need to hide now. Can you help me?" Flame mewed.

Maisie crouched back down again and looked into Flame's big emerald eyes. He was so tiny and helpless-looking. She felt a burst of protectiveness toward him.

"Of course I will. I'll take care of you. You can live with me and my parents," Maisie said, scooping him into her arms.

Flame rubbed his little head against her arm. "Thank you, Maisie."

"I'm going to love having you living with me. Just wait until I tell Mom and Dad about you!"

"No! You must tell no one my secret!" Flame reached up and touched her chin with one tiny, brown tabby paw. "Please promise, Maisie."

Maisie looked down into his serious little face. With his long, soft fur, striking tabby markings, and bright green eyes, he was the cutest kitten she had ever seen. She couldn't let him down. "All right. I promise. I'll just say you're a stray," she agreed.

Flame swished his bushy tail and began purring loudly. "That is good. Thank you, Maisie."

"Of course you can keep him!" Mrs.
Simpson said with a smile, when Maisie
finished explaining where she had found
the tiny kitten. She was in the kitchen
making ham sandwiches. "He's absolutely
gorgeous!"

Maisie smiled. She knew her mom
and dad would be fine about Flame
staying.

Mr. Simpson patted Flame. "What do

you know . . . a stray kitten turning up like that, just as we're moving in. He must be a good-luck token. Maybe you should call him Lucky."

"But he told me his name—" Maisie broke off. She was going to have to be a lot more careful about keeping Flame's secret. "I um . . . mean, I've already decided to call him Flame," she said hurriedly.

"Well, I think that suits him," her mom said. "I bet Flame's hungry. Kittens need to eat lots of small meals, you know. Why don't you see what you can find for him to eat?"

Maisie cut up a small slice of ham and poured some milk for Flame to drink. It wasn't much of a meal, but later she'd go to the store to get some cat food.

Flame chomped the ham and then lapped up the milk, purring loudly.

After lunch, Maisie took Flame upstairs. She laid an old sweater on her comforter and then lifted Flame onto it. He kneaded it into a soft nest with his front paws, and then curled up for a nap.

As Maisie stretched out on the bed beside the sleepy kitten, her face broke into a smile. She still couldn't believe this was happening. A couple of hours ago, she had been feeling lonely and missing her old friends. Now she had made her first new friend. In her wildest dreams, she had never expected him to be a magic kitten!

Chapter
THREE

Maisie had been having the most magical dream. She opened her eyes to find sunshine pouring through the bedroom curtains.

Something padded up the comforter with light steps. Flame sat on her chest and gave her a whiskery grin. "Good morning, Maisie. I slept very well," he purred.

Her dream was true! A huge smile spread across Maisie's face as she cuddled Flame and stroked his silky brown tabby fur.

"Hello, you two! You look nice and cozy!" James Simpson poked his head around Maisie's bedroom door. "I'm going for an early morning walk along the beach. Do you want to come?"

"Can Flame come, too?" Maisie asked.

Her dad grinned. "Course he can. See you downstairs in two minutes?"

"You're on!" Maisie lifted Flame aside and then threw back the covers. Leaping out of bed, she pulled on some jeans, a T-shirt, and sneakers. "Come on!" she called to Flame, dashing down the stairs with Flame following her.

Her dad was waiting at the back door

with an old canvas bag looped over his
shoulder.

"Is Mom sleeping in?" Maisie asked
him.

He shook his head. "She's already
in the old candy store, stripping some
woodwork. We'll come back and make her
breakfast, as a surprise."

"Okay," Maisie agreed.

Flame trotted after Maisie, as she
and her dad went outside and down the
steps to the beach. The tide was out, and
the sea was a gleaming silver line in the
distance.

They walked down to where the tide
had washed up bits of seaweed, plastic
bottles, shells, and other stuff. Flame
sniffed around, crunching up bits of dead
crab and enjoying the interesting smells.

"Yuck! I wouldn't like your breakfast,
Flame!" Maisie whispered, pulling a face.

Flame purred, chewing.

Her dad began sorting through a big
pile of seaweed.

"What are you looking for?" Maisie
asked him.

"I'll give you one guess."

"Bits of driftwood?" Maisie said.

"Got it in one!" her dad replied.

Maisie grinned at him. Her dad was amazing at carving birds and small animals out of small pieces of wood. She knew he planned to make some new statues from pieces of sun-bleached driftwood and sell them in the new gallery.

As Maisie drew closer to the rocks where she had found Flame the previous day, she saw a tall boy poking around in the rock pools. The boy glanced up and saw her. He smiled and waved.

Maisie climbed a steep bank of sand, which had blown against the rocks. Flame scrambled after her, but his short legs sank into the soft sand. Maisie picked him up and tucked him under one arm.

"Hi. You must be new around here.

I'm Joel Denning," the boy said with a
friendly smile. He had floppy brown hair
and wore a red T-shirt, cut-off jeans, and
battered sandals. He looked about twelve.

"Hi, I'm Maisie Simpson. I just
moved here with my parents. That's my
dad back there. We moved into that
house," Maisie said, turning and pointing
back up the beach.

"Oh, okay. I noticed that someone had moved into the old cottage. Hey, that's a really cute kitten you've got there," Joel said, noticing Flame peeking out from under Maisie's arm. He reached out to stroke Flame.

Flame purred as Joel rubbed the top of his head.

"Yes. His name is Flame. I . . . haven't had him long," Maisie told Joel. "Do you live nearby?"

Joel nodded. "Just down the road from you."

James Simpson strolled up to the rocks. He smiled at Joel. "Hello there. Found anything special?"

"Anemones, sea snails, a few crabs," Joel replied. "I was hoping to find a sea cucumber."

Maisie grinned. "Yeah, right! Good joke."

"No, really," Joel said seriously. "You can find amazing stuff. I keep a record of everything. See?" He produced a crumpled notebook from his pocket and held it up. "I write up my notes when I get home." He flashed Maisie and her dad a grin. "My dad thinks I know more about animals and plants than I do about people!"

Mr. Simpson laughed and glanced at Maisie. "Maybe you'll spend more time outdoors now that we live near the sea, instead of playing *Eagles and Hawks* for hours at a time."

"Da-ad!" Maisie groaned, turning bright red. He could be so embarrassing sometimes.

"What's *Eagles and Hawks*?" Joel asked, puzzled.

"It's a PlayStation game," Maisie said, amazed that Joel hadn't heard of it.

"Oh, right. I'm not really into computers." Joel seemed to lose interest but then his face brightened. "The best rock pools are at Smuggler's Cove. I'm going there tomorrow. I can show you both if you like."

"Thanks, but I've got a lot of work to do at the house," Mr. Simpson said. "Why don't you go with Joel, Maisie?"

"I . . . um, don't know . . .," Maisie began. She wasn't sure how much fun poking around in pools could be, but maybe it would be better than painting or unpacking, especially if Flame came, too. "All right, I'll come," she decided.

"Great!" Joel said, beaming. "I'll come get you in the morning."

"You'll be careful, won't you?" Maisie's mom called from the kitchen the following day, as Maisie dashed into the hall.

Joel was waiting at the open front door. "Don't worry, Mrs. Simpson. I know this part of the coast like the back of my hand," he shouted into the house. He wore hiking boots and had a sleeveless jacket with lots of zipped pockets over his shorts.

Without waiting for Maisie to come out of the house, he turned and began running down the road.

Maisie put her shoulder bag on the floor. "Can you jump inside, Flame? It might be a long walk."

Flame leaped into the bag with a swish of his tail, and Maisie shouldered the bag and hurried after Joel.

"Hey! Wait for us!" she called.

"Us?" Joel turned around with a puzzled look on his face and then noticed Flame's head sticking out of her bag. He frowned. "Why did you bring that kitten? You'll have to take it back."

"I'm not leaving Flame behind. Where I go, he goes!" Maisie said firmly.

"Well, fine then," Joel said grudgingly. "But make sure you take care of him. I don't want him getting in the way when I'm rock-pooling."

"He won't!" Maisie said. "Flame's a very unusual kitten. He's ma—I mean, he understands every word I say."

"Sure." Joel rolled his eyes before setting off again.

Maisie was starting to think this was a mistake. Joel had seemed friendly the day before, but today he was treating her as if she was a little kid.

She fell into step with him as they turned into a lane and took the cliff path. As they walked along, Joel pointed out tiny islands and told her the names of different rock formations.

Maisie was impressed. She had to admit that Joel knew a lot about this area. She could see that Flame was enjoying himself. He purred as he looked out of her bag at the sea and sniffed the salty air.

After about fifteen minutes, the path sloped downward until the cliff was more of a steep slope. Joel paused near some large flat rocks and boulders, above a small cove.

Looking down, Maisie saw a semicircular beach, surrounded by dramatic rocks. "Wow. Look at that. What an amazing place," she whispered to Flame.

Flame nodded.

"This is Smuggler's Cove. Wreckers used to lure ships onto those rocks and then steal the cargo," Joel said, pointing to where the surf was crashing onto some jagged black rocks that stretched out to sea. "There's a cave a bit farther along, where they hid their stuff."

"Really?" Maisie said, shuddering. The sunlit cove suddenly seemed sinister and unwelcoming.

Joel glanced at her pale face. "You

don't need to be scared. That was a long
time ago," he scoffed.

"I'm not scared," Maisie said defensively.

"Good. Because I don't want to
turn back now," Joel said. "We can take
a shortcut down by climbing over these
rocks. There's an easier way down, but it's
another ten-minute walk along the cliff
path."

Maisie leaned over a bit. Her tummy clenched as she looked down.

"I'll go first," Joel said, jumping onto the first rock, and then he glanced back at Maisie. "On second thought, it's a bit steep if you're not used to it, especially if you're wearing sneakers and carrying that kitten. You'd better come down the easier way. Just follow the path. You can't miss it—follow the signs to Smuggler's Cove."

"But aren't you coming with . . ." Maisie began.

Joel didn't reply. He was already scrambling down over the rocks.

Maisie stared down at him. She couldn't believe he had just left her to find her own way down. "That's just great!" she said to Flame.

Flame pricked up his ears and looked at her.

Maisie watched as Joel jumped down onto the small beach and then turned to look up at her and Flame. "Are you still there? Hurry up. I'll be just over here!" he called, waving, before turning around and disappearing out of sight behind a big rock.

Maisie clenched her fists. "Ugh! I've had about enough of Joel Denning. I'm climbing down there after him. How hard can it be? Hang on, Flame. Here we go."

Steadying her shoulder bag with one hand, she stepped down onto a large flat rock. Moving slowly and reaching for firm handholds, she climbed down backward. This was easier than it looked. Now she was almost halfway down.

But on the next rock, her shoe skidded and she slid toward the edge. She grabbed at a nearby rock to steady herself.

"Oh!" Maisie gasped as the rock moved under her hand and she lost her balance. She scrabbled for a foothold, but her foot slipped again and she found herself kicking out at thin air.

Chapter
FOUR

Time seemed to stand still. Flame
sprang out of the shoulder bag and landed
on the rock above Maisie.

His long brown tabby fur glittered
with sparks, and his whiskers crackled
with electricity. A warm tingling feeling
flowed down Maisie's spine.

Flame raised a tiny paw and a fountain
of bright silver sparks shot toward Maisie.

They swirled around her like a snowstorm.

"Oo-oh!" Maisie cried as her whole
body slid backward. She screwed her eyes
shut and prepared herself for a very painful
landing.

But she didn't fall. Instead, Maisie felt
herself sinking down slowly and gently.
Her eyes shot open and she realized that

she was encased in a big sparkling bubble. The bubble, with Maisie inside, landed on the beach. It bobbed up and down gently before settling and then disappeared with a faint pop!

Flame sprang down and landed beside Maisie. Every last trace of sparks had faded from his fur.

Maisie's knees suddenly gave way and she sat on the sand. Although she was safe now, she still felt shaken up.

Flame jumped into her lap. "Are you hurt?" he mewed anxiously.

"No. But only thanks to you. You were amazing, Flame! I didn't know you could do that! Thanks for saving me," she said, kissing the top of his silky little head.

"You are welcome," Flame purred.

Joel appeared from behind the rock. His eyebrows lifted in surprise when he saw Maisie sitting on the sand. He marched toward her, a fierce frown on his face.

"You went and hurt yourself, didn't you? I told you not to climb down!" he shouted.

Maisie felt her cheeks reddening with anger. "You just left me up there by myself!" she shouted back.

"Because I thought you might fall, you stupid kid!" Joel snapped.

Maisie lost her temper. She jumped to her feet and put her hands on her hips. "You're just a fat-headed idiot who likes ordering people around! I wish I hadn't come. I'm going home, right now!" she yelled.

Joel's mouth dropped open as Maisie turned on her heel. "Fine! See if I care," he called after her.

Tears of anger pricked Maisie's eyes as she found the path and stormed up the shallow rocky slope to the cliff path.

Flame scampered over the rocks and gullies, trying to keep up. He gave a frustrated little *meow* as he struggled to climb out of a gap between two rocks.

Maisie slowed down and lifted him into her shoulder bag. "Sorry, Flame," she apologized. "I didn't mean to march off like that."

She put her hand inside her bag and stroked his long soft fur as she walked along. Thank goodness she had Flame for her friend, because it didn't look like

she had any others now.

Maisie had just about calmed down by the time she and Flame reached home.

She sneaked quietly into the house, hoping to avoid awkward questions about why she was back so early.

Luckily her parents were still working
in the old store.

Her heart lifted when she saw
the computer set up on a wooden
desk in the corner of the living room.
She went to turn it on, but nothing
happened.

"Oh, great," she murmured. "I still
can't find out if Jane and Nina want to
be my friends." It felt so weird not to
be in touch with them.

Her dad came into the room and
saw her standing by the computer. "Hi,
honey. I'm afraid it's not working yet.
The computer man can't come to set
up the Internet out for a few more
days. How was Smuggler's Cove?"

"Okay. But a bit creepy, too," she
replied. "Joel said that wreckers lured

ships onto the rocks so they could rob
them."

"Where's Joel? Did he come back
with you?"

"No. I don't know where he is,"
Maisie said vaguely. "What's for lunch?"
she asked, changing the subject.

Her dad gave her a questioning look,
but didn't say anything.

"I wonder who that can be," Maisie
said to Flame later that afternoon as she
went to answer the front door.

Joel stood there with his hands
behind his back and a sheepish look on
his face. There was a girl with him. She
was small with short brown hair and
a pretty, round face and looked about
eleven years old.

Maisie blinked at them in surprise. She hadn't expected to see Joel again so soon. "What do you want?" she said stiffly.

"Er . . . hi," Joel said awkwardly. "This . . . um, is my sister, Louise."

Louise smiled at Maisie, her brown eyes sparkling. "Hi. Joel told me that you two had a fight this morning. He can't help being an idiot sometimes. It's because he's so crazy about wildlife. He thinks everyone should take it as seriously as he does." She grinned and nudged her brother. "Give them to her."

"All right, I was just going to!" Joel blushed and held out a pair of battered hiking boots. "These don't fit me anymore. I thought you might be able to use them for climbing rocks and stuff.

They're better than sneakers. And . . .
um, sorry about yelling at you earlier,"
he mumbled.

Despite herself, Maisie smiled. "That's
okay," she said as she reached for the
boots. "I'm sorry, too. I shouldn't have
lost my temper. Thanks for the boots."

"Thank goodness for that!" Louise
gave her brother a friendly shove and
then turned back to Maisie. "Now we
can all be friends. You and I are going to
be in the same class at school, you know."

"Are we?" Maisie said, liking Joel's
forceful sister more every minute. School
was certainly going to be interesting
with her around.

Louise looked down to where Flame
was standing by Maisie's ankle. Her eyes
lit up.

"Oo-ooh! What a gorgeous kitten. Can I pick him up?"

Maisie nodded. "But be careful. He's very small."

"I will. Don't worry." Louise bent down and scooped up Flame. She held him close to her chest and scratched him

gently under his chin. "Hello, you," she crooned.

Flame purred loudly and closed his eyes with pleasure.

Seeing that Flame felt secure, Maisie relaxed. She suddenly remembered her manners and opened the front door wide. "Why don't you both come in? I'll show you around and you can meet my mom and dad."

Louise stepped inside, still carrying Flame. "I thought you'd never ask!"

Maisie took Joel and Louise through to the old store where her parents were working and introduced them. "Look what I have. Joel gave them to me," she said, holding up the boots.

"That was very nice of you, Joel," Mrs. Simpson said, wiping her hands on a cloth. Joel blushed. He looked at the half-painted walls, wooden shelving, and bare floorboards. "It looks really different in here. Lighter and sort of . . . bigger."

"That's because there's no brown wallpaper or counter with musty newspapers, and no shelves with jars of sticky old candies," Louise said.

"Is that how it used to be? The old store sounds like a nightmare," said Mr. Simpson.

Joel and Louise laughed.

Maisie smiled at her parents. They were so good at making people feel at ease. She showed her new friends the rest of the house and then brought them back to the kitchen. They sat at the table. "Would you two like to stay for dinner?" she asked Joel and Louise.

Louise answered. "Thanks, but we better get back. Mom will be expecting us. Come on, Joel."

Maisie picked up Flame, who was curled up on her lap, and went to the door. "Bye. See you later!" she called as Joel and Louise left.

"We're going on a bike ride to Smuggler's Cove tomorrow and having a picnic with us. Do you want to come?" Louise said.

"You can wear your new boots," Joel encouraged.

As Flame gave an extraloud purr, Maisie grinned. "We'd love to!"

Chapter
FIVE

Maisie's hair streamed out behind her as she rode her bike the following morning.

Flame was in the basket attached to the handlebars. He leaned forward, his nose twitching as he sniffed at the exciting smells.

Maisie could see Joel and Louise up ahead. They were having a race to see who could reach the top of the hill first.

"I won!" shouted Joel, waving both arms in the air.

"Only because you have longer legs than me!" Louise cried. She turned around and biked back toward Maisie. "Almost there now. Smuggler's Cove is just around the headland."

"Great," Maisie said, pedaling hard as

Louise wheeled around again and sped after her brother once more. "Phew! Those two are some double act! I can hardly keep up with them!" she said to Flame.

Flame nodded, his bright emerald eyes sparkling. "Are we a double act, too?"

"We're the best ever!" Maisie said, feeling her heart swell with affection for the tiny kitten.

Smuggler's Cove had a picnic area on the cliff top. There was a small parking lot and a kiosk selling ice cream and drinks. Maisie lifted Flame out of the basket and then chained her bike up. Joel and Louise chained their bikes next to hers.

They sat on the grass to eat. The food was delicious, and Maisie ate hungrily.

She broke off pieces of her cheese
sandwich for Flame.

Joel was wearing his sleeveless jacket
with all the pockets. He sprawled on his
stomach to eat his chips. He'd almost
finished them when Louise jumped on
him. The chips shot everywhere.

"Hey! I hadn't finished those!" Joel
complained.

"Tough! You have now!" Louise said, giggling as she wrestled with her brother and tried to stuff grass into his mouth.

Maisie laughed. They were completely crazy. She hoped that they didn't decide to start on her!

After a few minutes, Joel and Louise sat up. Joel's jacket and Louise's T-shirt were covered in grass stains.

"Let's go and explore the caves," Joel suggested, shaking his head to get grass out of his hair.

"Do you think we should? Maisie might be scared," Louise panted, her brown eyes gleaming mischievously.

"Scared? Why would I be?" Maisie asked.

"Because of the legend," Louise

said, winking at her brother. "A smuggler was trapped inside the cave by the rising tide. Sea monsters swam up and dragged him away. Sometimes you can still hear his screams."

"I really believe that!" Maisie scoffed, laughing.

But even though she knew Louise was just teasing, she had a horrible squirmy feeling in her tummy. In her imagination, she could hear the bloodcurdling screams echoing around the lonely caves.

"Shut up, Lou, you're scaring her," Joel said. He got up and started walking down the grassy slope.

"Aw, she's not scared! Are you?" Louise said, beckoning to Maisie and Flame. "Come on, let's go!"

Flame trotted along at Maisie's heels
as she made her way down to the small,
sheltered cove. They had to scramble over
seaweed-draped rocks at the mouth of the
cave.

Maisie frowned as she entered the
shadowy cave. It was very dark at the
back, where the sunlight didn't reach.
Rocks were spread over the cave's sandy
floor. Small pools of cold, dark water were
dotted among them.

"Come on, you guys!" Joel called from
deep inside.

"We're coming! Hold your horses!"
Louise shouted, disappearing into the
shadows.

Maisie told herself that there was
nothing to be scared of as she went
farther into the cave after Louise and Joel.

"Are you all right, Flame? Do you want me to pick you up?" she whispered.

"I am fine, thank you, Maisie," Flame answered, placing each tiny brown tabby paw with deliberate care as he followed her over the rocks. Silver sparks shone faintly in his long silky fur.

Maisie shivered. It was getting chilly and smelled of damp and old seaweed. Every slight sound seemed magnified and spooky. There was no sign of Joel or Louise. She was really glad she had Flame with her.

Maisie was thinking of turning back, and risking being teased for being too chicken, when she noticed the natural shelves in the cave walls. There was a lot of driftwood there, washed up by the high tide when it filled the cave.

"Wow! Look at all that amazing wood. Dad would love it for his carvings," she said to Flame.

"Maybe you could tell him it is here, and then he can come and get it," Flame purred.

"Better than that, I'll take some

back for him as a surprise!" Maisie said.

She clambered toward the side
of the cave and began collecting
driftwood. Flame watched her from
where he sat on a rock beside a large
pool behind her.

"Who-oo-ooh!" Suddenly a terrible
wail rang out, echoing around the cave
creepily.

"Oh!" Maisie gasped, as her heart
missed a beat. It was the drowned
smuggler!

Then things seemed to happen
all at once. Maisie heard Joel and
Louise scream with fear, and then their
footsteps rang on the rocks as they
pounded toward her.

Just as Joel and Louise came into
sight, Flame screeched with panic.

Maisie turned to see him scrabbling for a pawhold on the seaweed. As she watched, he fell with a sickening splash into the pool.

Chapter
SIX

"Flame!" Maisie cried in horror. Dropping the driftwood, she sprang toward the rocks.

"What happened? Where is he?" Joel shouted, rushing up with Louise close behind him.

"He's under the water!" Maisie pointed at the pool, her heart pounding.

Flame's tiny head suddenly appeared.

He paddled desperately, his paws sending out ripples as he tried to keep his head above water.

"Swim to the side, Flame! You should be able to climb out," Maisie urged, hoping that the other two wouldn't realize that Flame actually understood.

Flame mewed and swam toward the side of the pool, where thick seaweed from the rocks draped into the water. He tried to catch hold with his claws, but it was no use and he slipped back in.

"He can't get out. He'll drown!" cried Louise.

Maisie felt desperate. She realized that Flame couldn't use his magic without giving himself away. Before she could think twice about it, she stepped forward and launched herself into the pool.

She gasped with shock as the icy water rose almost up to the tops of her thighs, and a dreadful pain shot up her leg. She had twisted her ankle on a submerged rock.

A wave of sickness washed over Maisie, but she gritted her teeth. Flame had sunk for a second time. She plunged her hands beneath the water and felt around.

"Got you!" she cried as her fingers closed over wet fur.

She lifted Flame up triumphantly

and held him to her chest. Shivering and whimpering with cold, Flame clung to her soaked T-shirt.

Joel and Louise leaned over to help Maisie clamber out of the pool. Trying not to put any weight on her twisted ankle, she crawled onto the rocks on her hands and knees.

Still holding Flame, Maisie managed to sit up. Her ankle throbbed with a dull ache, and she was shivering from head to foot. She bit her lip as a small groan escaped her.

"What's wrong? Are you hurt, Maisie?" Louise asked with concern.

"She's probably just cold. What did you jump in for, you idiot?" Joel scolded Maisie.

"Shut up, Joel! And give her your

jacket," Louise ordered, glaring at him.

Joel quickly took off his jacket and
spread it around Maisie's shoulders. As
soon as Flame was covered up, Maisie
felt sparks igniting in his fur and gently
prickling her fingers.

A familiar, warm tingling flowed down her spine. She felt deep, soothing heat spreading all over her body until her shivering gradually stopped. She gasped as the pain in her ankle increased for a second and then it seemed to pour away, like water down a drain.

Flame snuggled up to her, his tiny body warm once more and his silky fur as soft as velvet. As every last spark faded, his whole body vibrated with his purring.

"Stay with Maisie, Louise, I'll run and get help!" Joel cried.

Maisie realized that what had felt like minutes passing, while Flame performed his magic, had actually only been seconds. "No! Wait!" she called after Joel. "I'm feeling much better now. And Flame's okay, too. Let's just keep this between

ourselves. If my parents hear about this, I'll
be grounded until school starts!"

"You've got a point," Joel agreed.
"Our parents won't be too thrilled, either.
I'm the oldest, so I'll get the blame for
bringing you here."

"But are you sure you're all right?" Louise looked closely at Maisie and Flame. "I don't get it. You're hardly even wet. It's like magic," she said in amazement.

Maisie smiled to herself, wishing she could tell them how wonderful Flame really was. She sighed as she thought about how she could never tell anyone. "I'm fine," she said firmly. "Come on. Let's go!"

"I just realized what might make that awful shrieking sound," Joel said, as they retraced their steps back to Smuggler's Cove. "The wind blowing through a hole in the top of the cave."

"Now he tells us!" Louise said, rolling her eyes and giving her brother a punch on the arm.

"Ow!" Joel rubbed his arm and took a pretend swing at his sister.

Maisie bit back a grin as Joel and Louise squabbled. At least things were back to normal.

As she lifted Flame into her bike's basket, she bent over and whispered, "Are you okay now?"

Flame licked her chin with the tip of his rough little tongue. "I am fine. Thank you for saving me, Maisie. You were very brave," he purred.

"I wasn't really. I just couldn't bear to think of anything happening to you," she whispered fondly.

She realized that it was true. She couldn't imagine not having Flame around. Maisie felt a pang at the thought that one day he would have to go back to his own world. She shuddered and decided that she wasn't going to think about that.

Chapter
SEVEN

A couple of days later, Maisie was helping her mom put books on shelves and stack china in cupboards.

Flame was curled up on the sunny living-room windowsill, dozing.

"A week's gone by already," Mrs. Simpson said. "It's only a few days before we open the new gallery."

"I know. Everything seems to be

happening at once!" Maisie said. The computer was also finally set up and working.

Maisie had discovered that Jane and Nina had sent her long e-mails and had both been worried when Maisie hadn't replied for a few days. Now she was in touch with her friends and they were sharing news and chatting just like always.

Maisie had been e-mailing last night and received some great news. Both of them, with their families, were coming down for the grand opening on the weekend. "I can't wait to show Jane and Nina Smuggler's Cove and introduce them to Joel and Louise."

Mrs. Simpson smiled, but she looked a bit worried. "It'll be great for you to have your old friends here. But I hope we'll have the gallery ready in time. There seems to be so much to do."

Maisie went over and gave her mom a hug. "Don't worry. Flame and I will help you. Won't we, Flame?"

Flame blinked at her with bright green eyes.

"You and your imagination, Maisie Simpson," her mom exclaimed. "You talk as if that kitten's capable of anything! Maybe I should give him a mop and a bucket!"

Maisie smiled inwardly, as a cute picture of Flame cleaning the floor with a tiny mop came into her mind. *If only you knew*, she thought.

Maisie and Flame were in the old
store by themselves the next day, helping
decorate it. Mrs. Simpson had gone into
town to buy food, and Mr. Simpson was
searching for a furniture shop.

"Go for it!" Maisie clapped her
hands as the brush rose into the air
and then dipped itself into the pot of
varnish with a flourish. It wiped itself

carefully on the rim before dancing
across the wooden counter, a comet's
trail of silver sparks shooting out
behind it.

"Must work hard, must work hard!"
the brush sang softly to itself.

"Decorating's much more fun
with you helping, Flame!" Maisie said,
giggling.

Flame sat on the floor, grooming
his twinkling brown tabby fur. He
looked up from nibbling his front paw
and grinned at Maisie. "I am glad I can
be of help!"

Maisie heard the sound of footsteps.
"Quick! Someone's coming!"

A spark shot out of Flame's paw
and the brush fell silent. It zoomed
back to the open varnish tin and laid

itself across the top. Every last gleaming silver spark disappeared from Flame's fur.

Maisie rushed over and picked up the brush, just as her dad came into the store carrying a flat cardboard box under one arm.

He blinked with surprise when he saw the brush in Maisie's hand. "Goodness me, you've been busy! You're doing a grand job on that counter," he said.

Maisie blew on her nails and polished them on her T-shirt. "Does that mean I can have an increase in my allowance?" she asked, grinning.

Her dad chuckled. "Nice try! I'll think about it! Especially if you help me assemble this cabinet. It's one of those make-it-yourself items."

Maisie groaned inwardly. The words "make-it-yourself" and "dad" put together could mean trouble.

If only she could think of a way of getting her dad to go out again for a little while. Flame would have the cabinet assembled in a few sparkly seconds. But Mr. Simpson was already rolling up his sleeves, a determined look on his face.

"Okay. Where are the instructions?" he murmured, tearing open the box.

Maisie's heart sank as she knelt on the floor and started to help her dad.

An hour and a half later, sections of the unmade cabinet and little plastic packets of screws and bolts were strewn all around.

Flame sniffed at one of the bags and batted it with one paw.

Maisie quickly rescued the screws as they skidded across the room. "No, Flame. Leave those alone, please," she scolded gently. She looked at her dad. "Maybe you should get Mom to help you when she gets back from shopping," she suggested.

"I think you're right," her dad said, exasperated. He stood up with a heavy sigh and mopped his forehead on his shirtsleeve. "I give up! Who writes these instructions, anyway? They should be sued!"

"Never mind, Dad," Maisie said, trying hard not to laugh. "It did look really complicated. I think Flame and I will go to the beach if you don't need us anymore."

"Good idea. Are you going to call Joel and Louise?" he asked.

Maisie shook her head. "They had to go shopping for school uniforms with their mom. Anyway, I've got Flame for company. He's the best friend anyone could have."

Mr. Simpson smiled and reached

down to pat Flame. "Have a good time, you two. And don't forget to keep your eyes open for any interesting bits of driftwood."

"Definitely," Maisie said. "Come on, Flame."

Flame scampered after her as she went into the house and out to the front garden. Her bike was leaning against the house wall. She wheeled it out onto the street.

Flame's forehead wrinkled in a frown. "I do not think we need the bike to go to the beach, Maisie."

"No. But we do if we're going to Smuggler's Cove," Maisie said. "Remember all that amazing driftwood we saw in the cave? They were huge pieces. I'm going to get some for Dad. I

bet he needs cheering up after that mess
with the display cabinet."

Flame nodded. "That is a kind
thought. Perhaps you should tell him
where you are going or ask him to
come, too?"

Maisie thought about it. She had a
feeling that if she mentioned Smuggler's
Cove, her dad would say it was too far
to go by herself. But if she didn't ask
him, he couldn't tell her not to go.

"We're all ready now. Let's just go,"
she decided. "We won't be long."

Flame mewed an agreement as she
lifted him into the bike's front basket
and they set off.

Rain clouds were gathering
overhead and there was a cool breeze,
but Maisie hardly noticed the weather

as she biked along the cliff path. It was
perfect, just being with Flame. He sat
up in front of her, his ears pricked and
his little front paws resting over the rim
of the basket.

The small parking lot at Smuggler's
Cove was almost empty. There were
no picnickers today, only a couple of
people sitting on a bench looking out
to sea. The girl in the ice-cream kiosk
was reading a book.

Maisie chained up her bike and set
off down the grassy slope to the cove
with Flame at her heels. They soon
came to the mouth of the cave and
carefully climbed over the rocks to get
inside.

Maisie couldn't suppress a shudder
as she stood on the cave's sandy floor.

There was a slimy green mark about
three feet high up the rocky sides, where
the water obviously had come up to
when the tide came in.

When they had last come here, it had
been a bright sunny day, but the cave
had seemed damp and spooky. Today, it
seemed even more shadowy and gloomy.

Maisie bit her lip, recalling Louise's scary tales of trapped smugglers being dragged away by sea monsters.

"Is something wrong?" Flame mewed.

"Not really. It's just this place. It gives me the creeps," Maisie replied. "Let's get some driftwood and go."

Flame nodded. Suddenly he sat up straight and peered intently into the cave, as if he could hear something.

"What is it . . . ?" Maisie began, and then she froze.

Muffled sounds reached her. A burst of hollow laughter swelled in the air, echoing off the cave walls at the back. It gradually got louder as if someone, or something, was coming closer.

Maisie's eyes widened as a strange figure loomed out of the shadows. It

seemed to have a round back and lots of
dark shiny legs. Her blood ran cold as
the weird creature crawled over the rocks
toward her.

Chapter
EIGHT

"Argh! M . . . Monster! Flame . . .
help . . . ," Maisie stammered.

She couldn't move. The stories were
true. Sea monsters really did live in the
cave!

Beside her, Flame hissed. Maisie saw
sparks in his fur and then was surprised
when they quickly went out as the figure
came into the light.

Maisie dared to look back at the cave.

Relief washed over her. It was six
teenage kids in wetsuits, holding their
dinghy above their heads. There wasn't any
monster after all.

Maisie gave a shaky laugh as the
teenagers ran past her and headed for the
cave's entrance.

"Hi!" they called, waving and laughing.

"Hi!" Maisie waved back.

She watched them put the dinghy down
into the shallow water washing around
the cave's entrance. Some of the teenagers
jumped in and the others dragged the
dinghy out of sight. Just as they disappeared
from view, one of them shouted to Maisie.

"Don't hang around in here. Watch out
for the . . ." Whatever else he said was lost
in the sound of the waves crashing on the
rocks in the distance.

As soon as they were alone, Maisie
turned to Flame. "Phew! I was really
scared for a minute! Mom always says my
imagination works overtime!"

Flame gave her a whiskery grin and
rubbed himself against her ankles. "I
thought it was a sea monster, too!"

Maisie bent down and patted him

affectionately. "Did you? I don't feel like such a wimp then! Come on. Let's get some driftwood!"

She climbed up to the natural rocky shelves and began collecting big pieces of the twisted, bleached wood. Her dad could make some fantastic carved birds from this. When she had enough to almost fill the bike's basket, she clambered back down onto the cave's sandy floor.

"Oh!" she gasped, looking down in dismay as cold seawater swirled around her ankles.

She looked back toward the cave's entrance and saw that the sea was washing up the sides of the rocks there. The tide was coming in fast. With a gulp, Maisie now realized what the teenagers had been trying to warn her about.

She suddenly remembered the high tidemark on the cave walls. How long would it be before the cave was flooded?

"We're trapped, Flame! We're going to have to swim for it!" she cried.

Maisie stared in horror at the entrance to the cave. The cold gray sea was flowing in ever faster. The thought of having to swim around the cove and back to the beach terrified her.

Sparks ignited in Flame's long brown tabby fur and his whiskers crackled with electricity. Maisie felt a familiar, warm prickling sensation down her spine.

"Follow me!" Flame's eyes glowed like green coals. With a shower of bright sparks, he leaped from rock to rock, speeding toward the cave's entrance and the rising water.

"Wait!" Maisie pleaded, hesitating. "I can't, Flame. I'm too scared!"

"Trust me!" Flame called and then he leaped into the cold, swirling water.

Maisie felt her whole body fill with a strange tingling. Her feet moved all by themselves and she found herself

running after him. A flash of energy
shot up her spine. She rushed forward to
the mouth of the cave, and her muscles
tensed as she sprang up into a mighty
leap.

In a flash, she dived straight into
the sea. With a flick of her powerful
tail and flippers, she cut through the
water. Her body had become strong and
streamlined and covered with smooth
gray skin.

Flame had turned her into a dolphin!

There was a rush of water against
Maisie's elongated face and she shot
through the waves in a stream of bubbles.
Shoals of silver fish darted aside as she
dived down. She used her flippers and
tail to steer herself back around to the
cove, avoiding the sharp rocks.

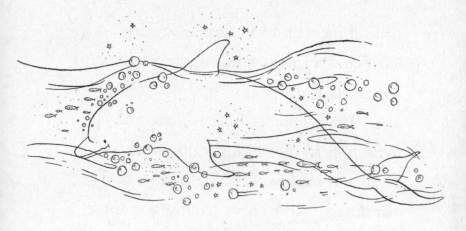

Leaping out of the water with sheer
excitement, Maisie performed a set of
somersaults, and then it was time to swim
toward the shore.

Maisie felt herself carried on the crest
of a wave. She coasted along at high speed,
like an expert surfer, riding the waves
rolling toward the shore.

As Maisie's feet touched the sandy
bottom, she stood up. Feet! She was a girl
again. Maisie ran up the beach, surprised

to find that she was completely dry.

Flame came bounding down the sand toward her.

"Wow! Thanks, Flame. That was awesome. I loved being a dolphin!" she said, her chest swelling with relief and happiness. "And I love having you for a friend. I hope you stay with me forever!"

Flame's emerald eyes twinkled with affection. "I will stay as long as I can," he answered in a soft purr that held a note of sadness.

Chapter
NINE

"Oh well. Dad's still going to have to go without his driftwood . . . ," Maisie commented, as she and Flame trudged up the beach and began the walk back toward Smuggler's Cove.

Flame's eyes twinkled, but he didn't reply.

Maisie's legs were aching by the time she and Flame had climbed the long

slope up to the parking lot. But as she
walked toward her bicycle, her face lit up.
The basket was filled to bursting with
some of the best pieces of driftwood!

"Oh, Flame, you're wonderful! You
think of everything," she said.

Flame gave a modest purr. "I try to!"

Maisie lifted him onto the wood

before unchaining her bike and biking home. She smiled to herself as she rode along, remembering the fantastic feeling of being a dolphin and swimming under the sea.

She knew she'd never forget the experience.

A few drops of rain began to fall as she biked up to Joel and Louise's house.

Their car was parked outside. Joel and Louise were just getting out. Both of them held plastic shopping bags. Maisie brought her bike to a stop.

"Hi! Have you and Flame been anywhere interesting?" Joel asked.

"Nah. Just collecting stuff for my dad," Maisie said vaguely. Joel wouldn't believe her if she told him the truth, even if she had been able to! "How

about you two? Did you have a good
time in town?"

"Duh! What do *you* think? We were
shopping for school stuff," Louise said,
pulling a face.

Maisie laughed. In all the excitement,
she had forgotten what Joel and Louise
had been doing. "Oh yeah! Poor you.

Do you want to meet up later?"

Joel looked up at the sky, where thick gray clouds were gathering. "There's not much point. It's going to pour. We can't go to the beach or go birdwatching or anything."

"But we could go to Maisie's house and play *Eagles and Hawks*," Louise suggested.

Maisie's head came up. "I never knew you liked playing computer games!"

"You never asked me. I love them. It's Joel who doesn't like them. He'd rather scribble in his old notebook about boring plants and creepy old insects."

Joel scowled at his sister. "Hey! Wildlife isn't boring!"

"Course it's not," Maisie said quickly, seeing another squabble brewing. "I like wildlife-watching *and* computers. Anyway, I've got to go home now. Why don't you both come over later?"

"Okay. See you!" Joel and Louise chorused as Maisie rode away.

"Those two!" Maisie said to Flame, with a grin. "I bet they'd argue that cornflakes were custard!"

A crack of thunder rumbled overhead. Lightning flashed across the sky outside Maisie's bedroom window as she entered her room.

"Flame? Where are you?" she said, peering around.

Strange. Flame usually followed her everywhere, but he had disappeared the minute lunch was over. She had searched for him downstairs, but he was nowhere in sight. Maybe he had come up here for a nap.

"Joel and Louise have just arrived. Aren't you coming downstairs to watch us play?" she said encouragingly.

Suddenly she noticed a small lump under her covers. As she lifted it up, she saw Flame's bushy tail sticking out from under a pillow.

"What's this—hide-and-seek?" she asked, smiling. But Maisie's face fell as Flame turned and looked at her with dull emerald eyes.

An awful suspicion was dawning on her. "It's your uncle's spies, isn't it? Have they come for you?"

Flame nodded, trembling all over. "I can sense them. They are nearby. But they may pass by if I stay very quiet and still," he mewed softly.

"But . . . what if they don't go past?" she gulped.

"I will have to leave, quickly, to save myself," Flame mewed.

"I understand," Maisie said in a small voice, her chest tightening with fear for him. It was horrible to think of Flame leaving, but far worse to think of him being hurt. She made herself answer calmly. "I'm staying here with you. I'll go and tell Joel and Louise I've changed my mind about playing games."

Flame shook his head and curled himself into an even tighter ball. "No, Maisie. You will only draw attention to me. Leave me here, please."

"All right." Maisie tucked the covers up high around the pillows. No one would know that a tiny kitten was hiding there. "I . . . I'll see you later," she said, going out onto the landing.

At least, I hope I will, she thought, slowly going downstairs.

There was an ache in her throat as she bit back tears. She could hardly believe that Flame might have to leave so suddenly and without even saying good-bye.

Chapter
TEN

Maisie waved good-bye to Joel
and Louise at the front door. "See
you tomorrow for the gallery's grand
opening!"

"You bet!" Louise said, grinning.

"Thanks for the game. Are you . . .
um, sure you're okay?" Joel asked, looking
concerned.

"I promise," Maisie said, smiling. She

felt bad that she'd been a bit quiet during the game, but she couldn't stop worrying about whether Flame would still be there.

The second they were gone, Maisie whipped around and ran up the stairs

two at a time. She slowly pushed open
her bedroom door, her heart in her
mouth.

"Flame!" she exclaimed.

He sat on the bed, cleaning his
whiskers. As soon as he saw Maisie, he
mewed a greeting. Jumping off the bed,
Flame ran toward her, his bushy tail
sticking up jauntily.

A huge smile spread across Maisie's
face as she picked him up and sat on the
rug to cuddle him. "I thought I'd never
see you again!"

Flame rubbed the top of his soft little
head against her chin. "My uncle's spies
have passed by. I am safe. For now."

"Good! I hope those horrible mean
things never come back!" Maisie said,
through gritted teeth.

Flame looked up with serious green
eyes. "They know I am close and they will
not stop looking for me. I may still have
to leave suddenly. Do you understand that,
Maisie?"

Maisie nodded, but she was
determined not to dwell on it. Her

wonderful, magical friend was still here, and that was all she cared about. "Let's go downstairs. Mom bought some cans of sardines the other day. Do you want some?"

Flame gave an eager little meow.

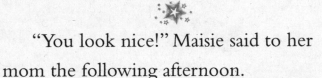

"You look nice!" Maisie said to her mom the following afternoon.

Mrs. Simpson had pinned her hair up. She wore sparkly earrings and a floaty blue dress. "Thanks, sweetie," she said, stretching plastic wrap over a stack of sandwiches.

"What time are people coming?" Maisie asked.

"In an hour or so, I imagine," her mom answered. "The invitations said after 4:00 p.m., but no one wants to be the first to arrive. There, the food's finished. Would you take these out for me, please?"

Maisie nodded. Flame padded after her as she carefully carried the heaped plate into the gallery.

Flame seemed just like his old self. There was no trace of his nervousness from the day before. Maisie had convinced herself that his enemies had forgotten all about him, and she smiled as she imagined the many adventures she and Flame would have together.

Mr. Simpson was in the gallery, setting out chairs. "Well? What do you think?" he asked, as Maisie put the plate on a table already piled with delicious food.

Maisie looked around at the wooden floor and old counter, which now shone like dark honey. Paintings hung on the spotless white walls, and colorful carved birds were on display in the modern cabinet.

"It's fantastic! Everyone's going to love it," she said proudly.

Her dad came over to give her a hug. "I think we're going to be very happy living here."

"Definitely!" Maisie said, grinning. "I wish Jane and Nina were already here, though. I hate waiting around when everything's ready."

Her dad ruffled her hair. "I think you've probably just got time to go down to the beach, if you're quick!"

Maisie flashed him a smile. She didn't need telling twice. "Come on, Flame!"

As she zoomed out into the back

garden, Flame ran along beside her. They
had almost reached the garden gate when
Maisie stopped suddenly.

Two powerful dark shapes were
climbing up the steps from the beach.
They gave a howl of rage as they smelled
Flame. They hurled themselves against the
closed gate with a crash!

Flame's enemies had found him!

"Save yourself, Flame!" she cried.

There was a bright flash. Where
the tiny kitten had been now stood a
magnificent young white lion and an
older gray lion stood next to him.

"Prince Flame! We must leave now!"
the gray lion growled urgently.

Flame turned to Maisie and his
emerald eyes crinkled in a smile of
farewell. "Be well, be strong, Maisie," he

said in a deep velvety growl as a rush of sparks swirled around him. And then he and the old lion were gone.

A harsh growl rang out as the dark shapes burst through the gate and then they, too, disappeared.

"Good-bye, Flame. I'll never forget you," Maisie said, her eyes filling with

tears. She was glad that Flame was safe.
One day he would be king in his own
world.

"Maisie! Oh, there you are. Jane and
Nina are here! And Joel and Louise just
arrived!" called Mr. Simpson from the
back door.

Maisie wiped her eyes. She knew she
was going to miss Flame a lot, but her
spirits rose at the thought of seeing her
old friends again. She had so much to talk
to them about. As she turned and went
into the house, she found herself smiling.

About the Author

Sue Bentley's books for children often include animals or fairies. She lives in Northampton, England, and enjoys reading, going to the movies, and sitting watching the frogs and newts in her garden pond. If she hadn't been a writer, she would probably have been a skydiver or brain surgeon. The main reason she writes is that she can drink cups and cups of tea while she's typing. She has met and owned many cats, and each one has brought a special sort of magic to her life.

Don't miss these Magic Kitten books!

#1 A Summer Spell

#2 Classroom Chaos

#3 Star Dreams

#4 Double Trouble

#5 Moonlight Mischief

#6 A Circus Wish

#7 Sparkling Steps

#8 A Glittering Gallop

#9 Seaside Mystery

A Christmas Surprise

Purrfect Sticker
and Activity Book

Starry Sticker
and Activity Book

Don't miss these Magic Ponies books!

Don't miss these Magic Puppy books!

Don't miss these Magic Bunny books!

#1 Chocolate Wishes

#2 Vacation Dreams

#3 A Splash of Magic